THE GRANDMASTER'S DAUGHTER

Dan-ah Kim

GREENWILLOW BOOKS

An Imprint of HarperCollins*Publishers*

The Grandmaster's Daughter
Copyright © 2021 by Danah Kim
All rights reserved. Manufactured in Italy.
For information address HarperCollins Children's Books,
a division of HarperCollins Publishers, 195 Broadway, New York, NY 10007.
www.harpercollinschildrens.com

The artwork was created with mixed media (gouache, acrylic, pencil,
colored pencil, cut paper, thread) and edited in Adobe Photoshop.
The text type is 22-point Schneidler BT.

Library of Congress Cataloging-in-Publication Data is available.

ISBN 9780063076907 (hardcover)
21 22 23 24 25 RTLO 10 9 8 7 6 5 4 3 2 1
First Edition

GREENWILLOW BOOKS

For Umma, Boram,
and Grandmaster Kim

In a small, quiet village
known for its persimmon trees
and pastel sunsets,
there is a modest dojang.

A school of martial arts.

Within its walls are
staffs, swords, and targets.

And often a small
girl named Sunny,
already a black belt.

The grandmaster's daughter.

When she's not practicing her forms,

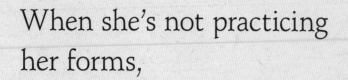

Sunny helps sweep the floors.

She waters the plants.

And feeds the cats.

She breaks up a street fight.

And a cat fight.

She gathers fruit for a snack.

She trains with her nunchucks.

They get twisted
and they twirl
and fly away!

Even black belts
mess up sometimes.

She teaches white belts how to kihap—

a breath, a shout;
power from the belly through the mouth!

Their kihaps grow bold enough
to wake the mountains!

The students have learned to use their skills only for defense.

They will protect one another.

The white belts
and blue belts,
the red belts
and yellow!

Sometimes they fly,

sometimes they fall.

But they won't give up
when they have battles to fight
and wounds to mend,
moves to learn and spirits to defend!

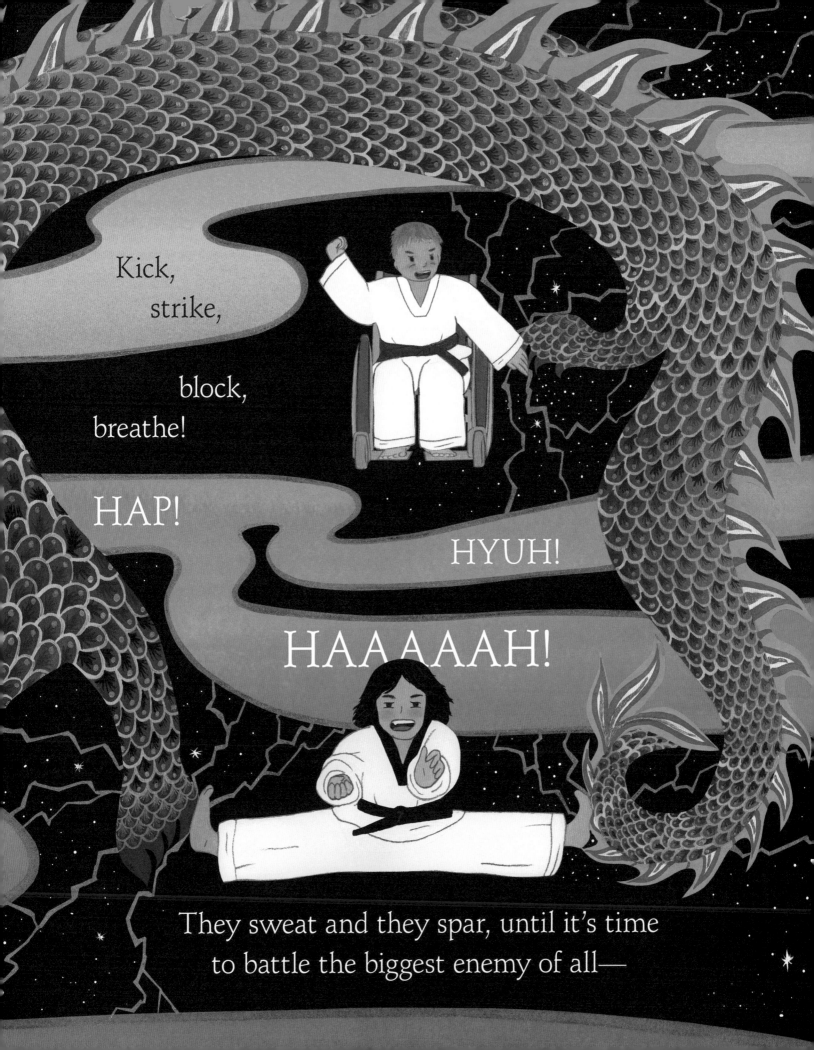

their growling . . .

stomachs!

Sunny offers peace with some snacks.

Everyone bows to say thanks.